Ellie The Elephant

Meets New Friends

I walked upon a

Big Hill Today

Oh my Goodness

It was such a Hurdle

I couldn't believe
My Eyes

I Met a Turtle

Hello Mr Turtle
What's your Name

I'm Tommy Turtle

Oh
I'm so pleased to meet
You

I'm Ellie

They Walked Together

Down a Dusty

Trail

Guess What Happened

They Met A

Snail

They both said

You're a Beautiful

Snail

We are very

Very Honored

to meet you

Thank you

I'm Sally Snail

I was just picking

some Flowers

from over

There

→

Guess What

Happened

Over There

?

I MET
A
RACCOON
THIS
AFTERNOON

Hello I'm Ronnie

I'm a Raccoon

I'm hiding in this

Garbage

Bin

I was looking for

Cake

But I saw a

Snake

HELLO
I'M SAMMY SNAKE

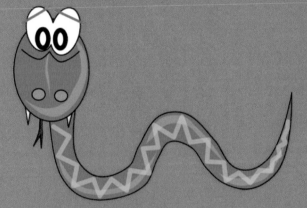

I HOPE I'M NOT

LATE FOR CAKE?

I saw a Raccoon

over there in a Bin

It seemed to me
He looked a bit Thin

I MET A MAN ALONG THE WAY

I SAID HELLO BUT HE

TURNED AWAY

THEN I REALIZED

HE WAS LOOKING FOR HIS

PUPPY

I was walking along

Singing a Tune

Then I saw that

Raccoon

Hello Ronnie Raccoon

I know it might be a bit late

But I know you were scared
of the Snake

So Iv'e brought you
a nice Big Cake

Oh thank you

Miss Ellie

I do appreciate that

Oh by the way did you see

That Cat

HELLO I'M ALLEY

THE CAT

I ran out of the
House
Trying to Catch that

Mouse

But I did See

That Hog

Talking to a

Frog

Hello I'm Hammy
Hog

I've just met

Freddie

The Frog

I looked up to the

Sky

I'm sure I saw a

Butterfly

Hello
I'm Bertie Butterfly

I Fly way up in the Sky

I WAS WATCHING ELLIE

SHE LOOKED SO EAGER

MABE SHE WAS LOOKING FOR A

BEAVER

Hello Miss Ellie
I'm Bucky Bea er
I just got some wood

That felll down from a
Tree

Very Pleased to meet you
Sir

I could hear something reselling

In the woods

Now I know it was you

Collecting that Wood

It was such a lovely

Day Today

Meeting New Friends

But as we know

All Good things
Must come to an End

So get Tucked into

Bed

It's time to say Goodnight

Don't Forget

To Tun off the

Light

Dedication

I dedicate this Book

To

Darlene O'connor

Sydney

Australia

Made in the USA
Monee, IL
27 September 2024

66805022R00021